From Crayons To Lipstick

Unveiling the mysteries of St. Joanna's convent, a boarding school in the hills of Kalimpong.

A Novella by Sonam Gadia

INDIA • SINGAPORE • MALAYSIA

Contents

A Personal Note from the Author

Dear Reader,

As you hold this book in your hands, know that you are holding a piece of my heart. Every word etched on these pages was written with love, stitched together with memories, and soaked in emotions that once kept me up at night.

This isn't just a story. It's a return to corridors that whispered secrets, windows that framed Kanchenjunga's quiet wisdom, and voices that shaped who I became- Through Ariana's journey, I hope you find fragments of your own your younger self, your silent bartles, your unspoken dreams.

Writing this book was both a reckoning and a release. And if it stirs something within you-if it makes you smile, cry, or pause-I will consider my purpose fulfilled.

If this story lingers in your heart even after the last page, do let me know. Your words inspire mine. Your love breathes life into my pen. And your belief will always be the reason I write again.

— *Sonam Gadia*

Pen O Pause

"Every Pause a Story, Every Story a Scar!"

Overall, "From Crayons to Lipstick" is a delightful and engaging masterpiece that will resonate with anyone who's experienced the joys and challenges of boarding life. The author's vivid descriptions of Kalimpong add to the story's charm, making it a must-read for fans of character-driven fiction.

— *Ipsita Banerjee*

Senior Chemistry Teacher & ICSE Examiner

Mahadevi Birla Shishu Vihar, Kolkata

Disclaimer

This is a work of fiction. Names, characters, and institutions are products of the author's imagination or used fictitiously. Any resemblance to real people or places is purely coincidental.

Dedication

To the Joannites—past, present, and future—whose spirit echoes through every misty corner of St. Joanna's Convent, may you always carry the courage to question, the strength to rise, and the bonds of friendship that time cannot break.

To my parents, whose belief in sending me to that distant convent nurtured my dreams and shaped my path.

To God and the universe, for guiding me through every corridor of discovery and silent prayer.

And to every boarding school soul—and every student everywhere—may you hold your stories close, for they are the light that guides us all, through the shadows and beyond.

Foreword

From the misty hills of Kalimpong to the pages of this book, every word is shaped by my experiences—both lived and imagined. As a student at a boarding school that seemed to hold countless secrets in its old walls, I've always been fascinated by the things left unsaid. This novel, From Lipstick to Crayons, is the result of years of reflection on the place that shaped me—the place I'll forever call home.

This story is not just mine. It belongs to anyone who has ever walked the long corridors of a school and felt the weight of silence, or who has questioned the truths they were told. From Lipstick to Crayons is a story of self-discovery, of unraveling the mysteries that have haunted me for years. It's a journey that takes us back to the familiar grounds of a school hidden in the hills, where the laughter and whispers of students collide with deep, buried secrets. It's about friendship, courage, and a truth that refuses to stay hidden.

After writing my first book, When the Moon Naps and Rainbows Smile, I realized that stories have the power to change perspectives, to heal, and to connect us to parts of ourselves we often overlook. This second journey with From Lipstick to Crayons was no different. It was a challenge, but also a gift, allowing me to explore new depths and tackle themes I hadn't approached before.

I want to extend my heartfelt thanks to all the readers who have supported me along this journey. Your words and encouragement inspire me to write, to explore, and to share these stories. As you turn the pages of this book, I invite you to remember your own childhood, your own school days, and the moments that have shaped you. Let's discover what's hidden behind the silence together.

Thank you for picking up this book. I hope it brings back memories, ignites questions, and leads you to uncover truths, just as it did for me. Let's embark on this journey together.

— Sonam Gadia

Preface

When I think back to my school days in the mist-covered hills of Kalimpong, I'm transported to a time of innocence, secrets, and hidden connections. My heart still beats to the rhythm of the bell that called us to our dorms and the silent whispers exchanged between friends as we navigated a world of rules, rituals, and unspoken truths. The corridors of my school were more than just brick and stone—they were a living, breathing part of me.

From Lipstick to Crayons is a reflection of those days. It's a story shaped by my experiences in a school that, like the one in these pages, stood atop a hill, gazing out at the majestic Mount Kanchenjunga. The memories of my boarding school, the friendships, the laughter, and the moments of solitude have always been intertwined with the mysteries I've carried inside me. It's these memories that gave life to the story of Ariana, who, like many of us, returns to face the unanswered questions that have followed her through the years.

This novel is more than just a walk down memory lane. It is an exploration of the hidden truths, the bonds formed through shared experiences, and the courage it takes to uncover what's buried beneath the surface. What I've learned over the years is that sometimes, the stories we carry with us are not just our own—they belong to the places that shaped us, the friends who stood by us, and the lessons we often forget.

The journey of writing this book was not just about telling Ariana's story, but also about revisiting the lessons of courage, friendship, and resilience that shaped me as a person. I owe a great deal to the school that shaped my life, and I hope this story resonates with anyone who has ever faced the weight of hidden truths or the longing for answers from their own past.

This book is my gift to all the girls who grew up in those halls, to the secrets they kept, and to the friendships that have withstood the test of time.

I hope it brings you back to those corridors, to the whispers of your own past, and to the truth you may have left behind.

— *Sonam Gadia*

Acknowledgements

There are stories that live in our hearts long before they find their way to the page. From Lipstick to Crayons was one such story—a mosaic of memories, emotions, and echoes from corridors that still whisper my name.

To the school nestled in the hills of Kalimpong—thank you for being more than just a backdrop. You were a living, breathing character in this journey. Though the name may be different, your spirit breathes through every page. I owe much of who I am today to the values, laughter, lessons, and friendships nurtured within your walls.

To all the girls who ever passed secret notes, laughed through lights-out, or cried into their pillows in shared dorms—this book is for you. Our stories may be different, but our hearts have likely walked the same paths.

To my family, thank you for your unwavering faith in my dreams, even when they didn't come with roadmaps. And to my little readers of When the Moon Naps and Rainbows Smile, you reminded me that stories, no matter how small, have the power to bloom into something beautiful.

To my friends who cheered me on, read early drafts, and offered both tea and truth when I needed them most—thank you for being my safety net and my sounding board.

A special thank you to Ipsita Banerjee, Senior Chemistry Teacher at Mahadevi Birla Shishu vihar, Kolkata, and ICSE Examiner, for her kind endorsement and belief in this story before it even met the world.

And finally—to the girl I once was, sitting by the dorm window, scribbling thoughts into a diary—this one's for you. You were always a storyteller.

With all my heart,

— Sonam Gadia

Prologue – The Letter That Waited

I almost missed it.

A letter, yellowed and faded at the edges, slipped between the pages of a book I hadn't touched in years. No name, no address—just a single sentence scrawled in slanted handwriting:

"Some truths never left the dorm."

That was all it took.

In an instant, I was back—beneath the misty skies of Kalimpong, where the air smells like pine and forgotten dreams.

Back in the convent halls that once echoed with our laughter, our secrets, our whispered promises.

Back where we exchanged words never meant to be spoken aloud, and where silence often said more than the loudest confession.

I had convinced myself that I had outgrown it—that I had packed away everything from those days—the letters folded in secret corners, the hidden friendships, and the regrets too heavy to carry. I had locked them all away in boxes that time had long since forgotten.

But the past has a way of finding its way out.

It doesn't ask permission.

It waits patiently until you're least expecting it.

And this time, I wasn't ready.

– Where Some Secrets Never Left

Dormitory

Cubicles

Secret Garden

*Only some knew
it was here...*

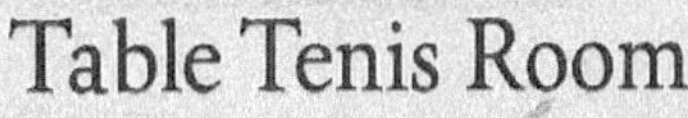

Basketball court

Table Tenis Room

Letter Rock

*Where secrets waited
in silence...*

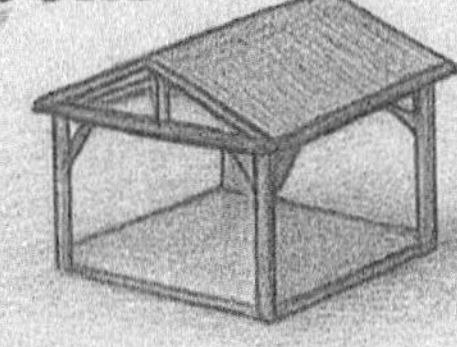

Pavilion

*Stories began–
whispered, shared, or silenced*

CHAPTER 1

First Bell Rings

--- • ---

The mist rolled over Kalimpong's hills, curling around rooftops and whispering through the pine trees. The crisp morning air smelled of damp earth and freshly baked bread from the convent kitchen.

Aru stood at the **iron gates of St. Joanna's Convent**, gripping the strap of her satchel. In front of her, the **red-bricked school building loomed tall**, its arched windows glinting in the soft sunlight.

"Another year," she thought. Another year of **strict rules, whispered secrets, and the ever-present thrill of growing up.**

"Come on, Ari!" Tara Chhetri whispered, tugging her hand.

The **morning bell rang,** loud and clear.

The girls lined up in their **navy-blue pinafores, white socks neatly folded down, blue ribbons tying back their hair.**

At the front of the courtyard, **Sister Vincent,** the respected headmistress, stood with her piercing gaze scanning the students.

"Welcome back, girls," she said. "This year, I expect great things from each of you."

Ariana smirked. *Great things? I have my own definition of that.*

As the school day began—the rhythmic scratching of pencils against notebooks, the murmured prayers before lunch, the faint creak of old wooden desks—Ariana's mind was elsewhere.

During **lunch break,** she and Tara sneaked into the **library,** where towering bookshelves stood like ancient guardians of forgotten stories.

That's when they **found it.**

A **red leather diary,** buried beneath a pile of dusty books.

Tara flipped it open. The ink was **old, faded**—but the words were chillingly clear.

"I know I shouldn't write this. But if something happens to me, someone must know the truth."

Ariana felt a **shiver** crawl up her spine.

Something told her that **St. Joanna's Convent held more secrets than anyone realized.**

CHAPTER 2

The Art of Rebellion

———•◦•———

If there was one thing every **St. Joanna's girl** knew, it was this:

- **No eating food from outside.**
- **No sneaking out of campus.**
- **No questioning the rules.**

But **rules were meant to be bent**—at least, according to Ariana.

The convent's **dining hall food** was simple—rice, dal, and a fresh vegetable curry, day after day. But what the girls truly **craved** was the **street food just outside the school gates.**

Tara sighed dramatically as she poked at her dal. "If I don't get a plate of **red aloo dum** today, I might actually cry."

Ariana grinned. "Then let's do it. **After choir practice.**"

Tara's eyes widened. "You want to **sneak out**? Are you insane?"

"Probably."

That evening, as the sun dipped behind the hills, **Ariana and Tara slipped through the side gate near the basketball court.**

The road outside was alive with **the aroma of momos, the sizzle of phumbi on hot plates, and the sight of steaming thukpa served on fresh lotus leaves.**

Ariana had just taken her first, **forbidden bite of lephing**—spicy, tangy, and absolutely worth the risk—when a voice cut through the evening air.

"Ariana Sen!"

Her heart **stopped.**

Sister Grace stood **two feet away,** arms crossed, eyes calm but firm.

Busted.

CHAPTER 3

A Lesson in Numbers & Nails

The **next morning**, Ariana walked into class, still thinking about the **red leather diary**.

But she didn't have time to think.

Because **Math class with Sir Abdul Kalam** was about to begin.

The Infamous "Red Liquid" Treatment

Before class, Ariana was sent to the **infirmary.**

"For what?" she asked, confused.

"For your own good," Sister Grace replied with a knowing look.

She **knew** exactly what that meant.

The **school infirmary**, a small sunlit room near the chapel, had one universal cure for everything.

Ariana barely had time to sit when the **nurse walked in, holding a tray.**

On it sat a **bottle filled with bright red liquid** and a ball of cotton.

Ariana groaned. "Oh no. **Not the red liquid!**"

"Ah, good old mystery medicine," Tara muttered beside her. "What's in it, anyway?"

"No one knows," Ariana whispered dramatically. "But rumor has it, if you put some on a broken leg, the leg will just… **disappear.**"

Tara **choked on her laughter** as the nurse dabbed a large amount of the **fiery red liquid** on Ariana's wrist.

It **burned. Instantly.**

"OW!" Ariana yelped.

"Good," the nurse said, satisfied. "That means it's working."

Tara smirked. "This school has **two cures**—red liquid for injuries, **saltwater for everything else.**"

At that moment, a younger student accidentally spat **her entire tumbler of saltwater onto her shoes.**

Sister Grace appeared out of nowhere, arms crossed.

"Gargle properly, child! It's for your own good!"

Ariana whispered, **"Gargle or die."**

Tara collapsed in **silent laughter.**

CHAPTER 4

Meet Me at Midnight

--- • ---

At **lunch**, a folded note slipped onto Ariana's tray.

She froze.

The handwriting was **old-fashioned, delicate—and very, very familiar.**

It was the **same as the writing in the red diary.**

Her hands trembled as she opened it.

It had only **four words.**

"Meet me at midnight."

Tara stopped walking. "No. Nope. We are **not** doing this."

Ariana smirked. "Or you're not. But I am."

"You're insane," Tara whispered.

"Probably."

That night, as the dormitory **slept**, Ariana **tiptoed into the corridor.**

And then—she **saw it.**

The **red leather diary,** sitting on the windowsill.

But this time, there was a **new entry.**

Her hands trembled as she flipped open the page.

"I knew you would come, Ariana Sen. Now, let's finish what I started."

Ariana **spun around.**

The hallway was **empty.**

But she could **feel it.**

Someone had been **here.**

Someone had been **watching.**

CHAPTER 5

The Midnight Secret

— ·•· —

Ariana didn't sleep that night.

The diary's words burned in her mind.

Someone had written to her.

Someone had been here.

Someone was **leading her to something.**

By the next morning, mystery took a backseat—because the **Annual Concert rehearsals** had begun.

The **assembly hall** buzzed with excitement.

Ariana adjusted her anklets as Tara whispered, "I bet the concert will be normal for once."

Ariana smirked. "I bet it won't."

Because **strange things were already happening.**

And **the diary's secret was far from over.**

CHAPTER 6

Monkey Business & Secret Snacks

———•———

Ariana had survived **midnight mysteries, Monday tests, and Sister Grace's punishments**—but nothing could prepare her for what was about to happen in Math class.

Sir Abdul Kalam, the most dramatic teacher at St. Joanna's Convent, had a habit of making bold declarations.

"I am the bravest man in this school!" he announced one morning, pacing in front of the blackboard. "Nothing—NOTHING—scares me!"

Ariana and Tara exchanged **amused glances.**

That very morning, a notice had been pinned up outside the **school office:**

"Students, be cautious. Monkeys have been spotted near the school grounds. Avoid keeping food outside windows."

If there was **one thing** that could **throw St. Joanna's into chaos**, it was a monkey invasion.

And Class 9C was about to experience it firsthand.

The Monkey Invasion – Class 9C

It started with a **loud thud** against the classroom window.

Then—a **furry, brown blur** leaped onto the windowsill.

A collective **gasp** rippled through the classroom.

The monkey **paused**, scanning the room like it was **choosing its next victim.**

Then, it **jumped straight into the class.**

What followed was **pure pandemonium.**

Books and bags went flying. Girls **screamed.** Desks **scraped against the floor.**

And in the middle of the chaos—Sir Abdul Kalam let out a shriek **so high-pitched, even the monkey paused for a second.**

The **man who had declared himself the bravest** had scrambled **onto his own desk,** clutching his duster like a shield.

"HELP! HELP! **CLOSE THE DOOR!**" he howled.

Ariana **had to physically hold Tara back** from collapsing in laughter.

"Get it out! **Someone get it out!**" Sir Abdul Kalam **wailed.**

Meanwhile, the monkey, completely **unbothered**, casually strutted across the classroom, grabbed an **unopened tiffin box,** and leaped back **out the window.**

The class sat in **stunned silence.**

Sir Abdul Kalam **slowly climbed down from the desk, dusting off his sleeves,** pretending none of that had just happened.

"Alright," he **cleared his throat**, regaining composure. "Where were we? Ah yes, quadratic equations…"

Tara **whispered to Ariana,** "This is the best Math class we've ever had."

Ariana smirked. "And the **bravest teacher.**"

The Secret Snack Smugglers

The monkey wasn't the **only** sneaky creature at St. Joanna's.

For **boarders,** getting food from outside was **strictly forbidden**—but that never stopped them from trying.

The hawker outside the school gates **sold the most delicious beef and veg patties, sweet buns, and hot jhalmuri.**

One afternoon, a girl from Class 10 **bravely decided** to make a purchase.

She handed her **money to a friend behind her**, who passed it to another, who passed it to another—until it **finally reached the hawker.**

She waited, stretching her hands behind her back to **receive her snacks.**

But instead of the **warm patties and buns**, she felt something **cold and stiff.**

She turned around—and nearly **fainted.**

Standing behind her, holding **all the snacks,** was a **Sister.**

The entire class **held their breath.**

The girl swallowed hard. "S-sister... that's... that's my friend's..."

The **Sister raised an eyebrow.** "Oh? Then let's take it to your friend **together.**"

BUSTED.

The **hawker operation was shut down**—until someone else dared to try again.

Basketball Rivalry: SJC vs. Dr.Grantham's Homes

Sports Day was exciting, but **nothing** compared to **basketball matches between SJC and Dr.Grantham's Homes.**

The rivalry was **legendary**—as thrilling as an **India vs. Pakistan** cricket match.

The court was **packed** with students, cheering at the top of their lungs "I scream,you scream,everybody scream for SJC"

"Let's go, SJC!" girls shouted, waving their **house flags.**

The **band boys from San Augustino School** were also in the audience, **some too focused on watching the players instead of the game.**

Tara nudged Ariana. "Why are they **cheering so much** for the SJC team?"

Ariana smirked. "Not the team. **The players.**"

The match was **intense,** the ball **flying back and forth across the court.**

With **only 30 seconds left on the clock,** the score was **tied.**

SJC had the ball.

Everyone **held their breath.**

The shooter **leaped, aimed, and—**

SWISH.

The ball **sailed through the hoop** just as the **buzzer rang.**

SJC WON!

The court **exploded** into cheers, stomping, and wild clapping.

Ariana and Tara **high-fived everyone in sight.**

This wasn't just a **win.**

This was **a victory for the entire school.**

Independence Day March & Band Heroes

At **St. Joanna's Convent,** Independence Day was **no ordinary celebration.**

Preparations started **two months in advance.**

Every day, students stood **house-wise, marching in perfect rhythm** under the watchful eyes of the PT teachers.

The **school band** was the **pride of the event.**

The drummers, flute players, and band conductor became **heroes for the entire month of August.**

Ariana, standing in her **house line,** watched as the **flute players practiced their notes,** the drummers tapped out beats, and the band **marched in sync.**

It was **exhausting,** but there was a sense of **pride and unity** in it all.

Little did they realize—these **small moments of discipline and teamwork** were **shaping them for life.**

The Mystery Deepens

Amidst the excitement of **sports, celebrations, and mischief,** Ariana hadn't forgotten about the **diary.**

She had spent days **reading through its pages,** but it was still **unclear who had written it.**

One afternoon, as she walked past the **prize table at the school fete,** something caught her eye.

A **small, red leather-bound notebook** sat among the books.

Her **heart stopped.**

Another diary?

She reached for it.

But just as her fingers touched the cover—

Someone **else grabbed it first.**

A **shadowy figure** in a school uniform.

Ariana looked up.

But before she could see their **face—**

They **turned and disappeared into the crowd.**

CHAPTER 7

The Social, The Letters, and a New Clue

— · ● · —

Ariana had faced **midnight mysteries, monkey mayhem, and secret snack missions,** but nothing could prepare her for the one event that **every girl at St. Joanna's both anticipated and feared—**

The School Social.

Every year, **St. Joanna's Convent** hosted a formal **social with the boys from San Augustino School.** Officially, it was a night of **dancing, polite conversations, and innocent fun.**

But **for the students—**it was **so much more.**

It was the one night where **letters** were exchanged.

The Secret Letters from San Augustino School

In the **days leading up to the social,** a familiar scene played out near the **school fences.**

Girls **hovered near the boundary wall,** pretending to admire the trees while **tiny folded notes** were **passed over from the boys on the other side.**

Tara smirked as she **tucked a tiny folded letter** into her pinafore pocket. "The tradition lives on," she whispered.

Ariana raised an eyebrow. "Should I be worried about what's inside?"

Tara grinned. "Depends. **If it's written in blue ink—it's casual. If it's in black ink—it's serious. If it's in red ink— someone is either madly in love or plotting revenge.**"

Ariana **rolled her eyes.** "And if it's in pencil?"

Tara **gasped.** "Then he's a **coward.**"

They **burst into laughter.** The **letter tradition** had existed for **decades**—even though it was **strictly forbidden.**

But as Ariana watched the **secret exchanges,** her mind went back to **a different letter.**

The **diary.**

Someone at school **knew about it.**

And she was going to find out **who.**

The Social Begins

The evening of the **social** was always **magical.**

The convent's **large assembly hall** was decorated with **fairy lights**, and **soft music** played in the background.

Girls stood in **small groups**, whispering and adjusting their ribbons. The boys from **San Augustino School** arrived, looking **equally nervous.**

Ariana, however, was only **half-interested.**

Her mind was elsewhere.

Tara nudged her. "Ari, are you even paying attention?"

Ariana snapped back to reality. "What?"

Tara **rolled her eyes.** "We have **one** night where we can actually talk to the **outside world**, and you're standing here like you're solving a murder case."

Ariana smirked. **"Maybe I am."**

She **glanced around the room, scanning the crowd.**

Somewhere in this hall was the person who had **taken the second diary.**

And she was going to **find them.**

A Mysterious Dance Partner

The music **changed** to a slow waltz.

One by one, **boys approached the girls**, asking them to dance.

Ariana wasn't **paying attention—**until a voice interrupted her thoughts.

"Would you like to dance?"

She **turned.**

A **tall boy** with neatly combed hair and **deep brown eyes** stood in front of her.

Ariana hesitated. "Uh—"

Before she could **refuse,** Tara **pushed her forward.**

"Of course she would!"

Ariana shot her a **glare** before reluctantly placing her hand in his.

As they stepped onto the **dance floor,** the boy spoke.

"You don't remember me, do you?"

Ariana **frowned.** "Should I?"

He **smiled slightly.** "We used to be in the same tuition class… years ago."

Ariana **blinked.** And then—she remembered.

"Neel?"

He nodded. "Took you long enough."

Ariana **couldn't believe it.**

Neel Mehra.

They had both attended **the same math tuition** when they were younger. She hadn't seen him in **years.**

But before she could say anything else, **Neel whispered—**

"I need to talk to you. It's about the diary."

Ariana's **breath caught in her throat.**

The **diary?**

She stared at him. **"What do you mean?"**

Neel **glanced around cautiously.** "Not here. **Meet me near the basketball court after the social.** I'll explain everything."

Ariana's **heart pounded.**

He knew something.

But could she **trust him?**

The Social Ends, The Mystery Deepens

As the evening came to a **close,** the girls said their **goodbyes** and walked back to their **dormitories.**

But Ariana's mind was **racing.**

Neel had **answers.**

And she was going to **find out exactly what he knew.**

CHAPTER 8

Secrets Under the Moonlight

The school corridors were **silent** as Ariana **slipped out of the dormitory**, her heart pounding.

She knew this was **risky.**

If a Sister **caught her sneaking out,** she'd be given **chapel duty for a month—or worse, have her social privileges revoked.**

But she **didn't care.**

Neel Mehra had answers.

And she was going to **get them.**

A Midnight Meeting

The **basketball court** was dimly lit by the **moonlight,** casting **long shadows** on the ground.

Neel was already there, leaning against the **old rusting goalpost,** his hands shoved in his pockets.

"You actually came," he said, smirking.

Ariana **crossed her arms.** "I don't waste my time. **Now talk. What do you know about the diary?"**

Neel's **smile faded.**

"It belonged to my sister."

Ariana's **stomach dropped.**

"Your… sister?"

Neel nodded. **"Her name was Riya Mehra. She was a boarder here—three years ahead of you. But something happened, Ariana. She left school suddenly… and no one ever talked about her again."**

Ariana **shivered.**

She had **never heard** of a **Riya Mehra.**

"But what does that have to do with me?" she asked, her voice **quiet now.**

Neel exhaled. **"Because Riya used to talk about a secret hidden in the school. Something she was trying to uncover before she left. And before she disappeared, she left her diary behind."**

Ariana **felt her blood turn cold.**

A secret?

"What kind of secret?" she demanded.

Neel hesitated, then shook his head. **"I don't know. But she always said, 'If something happens, someone will find the truth.'"**

Ariana **swallowed hard.**

The **diary.**

It had **found its way** to her.

She wasn't **imagining things.**

She was meant to uncover whatever **Riya had left behind.**

A Warning

Neel studied her face. **"Listen… I don't know how deep this goes, but be careful, okay? Some secrets are meant to stay buried."**

Ariana **lifted her chin.**

"Well, I don't believe in **buried secrets.**"

Neel **chuckled.** "Yeah. **I figured.**"

As Ariana **turned to leave,** Neel called out, **"Ariana, wait."**

She glanced back.

"Whatever happens next… don't trust everyone."

Ariana didn't reply.

But deep down, she **already knew.**

CHAPTER 9

Secrets Under the Grand Staircase

The note sat heavy in Ariana's pocket.

"You're closer than you think. Look under the grand staircase."

Who had left it?

What was waiting for her there?

The **grand staircase** at St. Joanna's wasn't just a staircase—it was a **landmark**. Generations of girls had **climbed its polished wooden steps**, their laughter and whispers etched into the walls.

But Ariana had never thought about **what lay beneath it**.

Until now.

A Midnight Mission

Ariana waited until the **dormitory lights** went out before she **slipped out of bed**.

Tara stirred beside her. **"Ariana...?"** she murmured sleepily.

Ariana hesitated. Should she tell her?

Tara had been her **partner-in-crime** for everything—**sneaking out, decoding the diary, breaking curfew.**

With a sigh, Ariana whispered, **"Fine. But if we get caught, you're taking the blame."**

Tara **grinned.** "Deal."

The two girls **tiptoed** through the **silent corridors,** their footsteps barely making a sound.

The **school at night** was a different world—the hallways stretched **longer,** the shadows **darker,** the silence **louder.**

When they reached the **grand staircase,** Ariana **exhaled slowly.**

It stood before them in the **dim moonlight,** its **carved wooden railings casting eerie shadows** on the floor.

Tara **hugged herself.** "Remind me why we're doing this again?"

Ariana crouched near the base of the staircase. "Because someone **wants us to.**"

She **ran her hands** along the **wooden panels,** searching.

Nothing.

Tara sighed. "Maybe this was just a prank."

But Ariana wasn't convinced.

She **pulled out her flashlight**, sweeping the beam across the dust-covered wood.

Then—

Her breath caught.

A **tiny, rusted keyhole**, almost invisible, was hidden beneath the **lowest step.**

Ariana and Tara **exchanged glances.**

"That's a **secret compartment,** isn't it?" Tara whispered.

Ariana **pressed against the panel.** It was slightly **loose.**

She **pushed harder—**

And with a soft **click**, the wooden panel **shifted open.**

Behind it was a **small, hidden compartment.**

And inside—

A **dust-covered envelope.**

Ariana's **hands trembled** as she pulled it out.

She opened it.

Inside was a **letter.**

A **very, very old letter.**

The Letter from the Past

The **ink was smudged with age**, but the handwriting was **elegant and deliberate.**

Ariana read it aloud, her voice barely above a whisper.

"To the one who finds this—

I don't know who you are. But if you're reading this, it means you've discovered what I couldn't. I was close—so close—but I had to leave before I could finish.

There is something hidden within these walls. A secret buried long before our time. And I fear that if it comes to light, not everyone will be happy about it.

Be careful. Trust no one.

And if you wish to know the truth…

Look inside the library archives."

*- **R.M.***

Ariana's **stomach twisted.**

"R.M.?" Tara whispered.

Ariana **swallowed hard.**

"Riya Mehra."

Neel's **missing sister.**

Ariana's Next Move

Ariana folded the letter **carefully**, her mind **spinning.**

First, she had found **the diary.**

Then, she had discovered **Neel's connection to it.** Now, she had a **letter from the past,** warning her about **something buried within the school itself.**

And the next clue?

It was waiting for her **inside the library archives.**

Tara groaned. "You do realize this means we have to **sneak into the library, right?"**

Ariana **smirked.** "Wouldn't be our first time."

Tara **sighed dramatically.** "Why do I let you drag me into these things?"

Ariana **tucked the letter** into her pinafore pocket.

Because the **mystery wasn't over.**

It was only just **beginning.**

CHAPTER 10

Shadows in the Library

The **next night**, Ariana stood outside the **library doors**, her pulse quickening.

St. Joanna's Convent was silent at this hour. The moonlight **cast long, eerie shadows** through the open corridors.

The library was tucked away beneath the **new building**, near the **table tennis room**—far from the dormitories and even farther from help **if they got caught.**

Tara **shivered.** "You do realize if we get caught, **Sister Agnes** will personally haunt us for the rest of our lives?"

Ariana **smirked.** "Then let's not get caught."

The library door was **locked**, as expected.

But Ariana had **planned ahead.**

She pulled out a **thin hairpin** from her pocket and **knelt beside the keyhole.**

Tara **raised an eyebrow.** "Since when do you know how to pick locks?"

Ariana **gave her a pointed look.** "You think I sneak out for **street food** without learning a few tricks?"

With a soft **click,** the door **creaked open.**

The scent of **aged parchment, ink, and polished wood** filled the air as they slipped inside, closing the door **behind them.**

Inside the Archives

The library was **vast**—even **more intimidating at night.**

Rows of **towering bookshelves** stretched from wall to wall, their **spines glistening faintly** in the dim emergency light.

Tara whispered, **"Alright, genius. Where do we start?"**

Ariana pulled out **Riya Mehra's letter** and reread the last line.

"Look inside the library archives."

She turned to Tara. **"The archives are in the restricted section, past the old reading room."**

Tara **groaned.** "Of course they are."

They **tiptoed** through the shelves, past the **tall wooden tables** near the entrance, and towards the **back of the library,** where a **wrought-iron gate** separated the restricted section.

Ariana **ran her fingers** along the gate's **cold metal bars.** It was locked with an **old-fashioned padlock.**

Tara crossed her arms. **"And what, you're a master thief now?"**

Ariana **smirked.** "Not quite. **Just resourceful."**

She pulled out a **small, rusted key** from her pinafore pocket.

Tara's **eyes widened.** "Where did you—"

"I borrowed it **from Sister Beatrice's desk."**

Ariana slid the key into the lock.

With a **soft click,** the **gate swung open.**

They stepped inside.

The Secret Files

The **restricted section** smelled even **older than the rest of the library**—like **dust, ink, and time itself.**

Ariana **scanned the shelves, searching.**

Then—

She **froze.**

A **thick leather-bound ledger** sat slightly **askew** on the third shelf.

Unlike the other books, it wasn't **covered in dust.**

Someone had touched it recently.

Ariana **reached for it and carefully opened the cover.**

The pages were filled with **neat, old-fashioned handwriting.**

She flipped through the first few pages.

They seemed like **ordinary school records.**

But then—

A **folded newspaper clipping** slipped out and fluttered to the floor.

Tara picked it up.

Her **face went pale.**

"Ariana… you need to read this."

Ariana **picked it up.**

Her **blood ran cold.**

The headline read: "Mysterious Fire at St. Joanna's Convent – 1952."

CHAPTER 11

Bath Time & Secret Notes

The **morning cleaning routine** at St. Joanna's Convent was as **predictable as the chapel bells**—and just as impossible to escape.

Every morning, students were assigned **cleaning duties.** Some had to sweep the **study hall,** others cleared the **main ground,** while Ariana and Tara—thanks to **Sister Agnes's secret grudge** against them—were **stuck with the new building.**

Tara dragged her broom behind her with an **exaggerated sigh.** "Another exciting morning of **cleaning dust that's just going to come back tomorrow.**"

Ariana smirked. **"Welcome to St. Joanna's. Where dust is eternal, but our suffering is scheduled."**

Tara shook her head. **"You should put that on the school brochure."**

They worked in **silence for a while,** the rhythmic **swishing of brooms** the only sound.

But Ariana's mind was **elsewhere.**

She couldn't stop thinking about last night's **discovery in the library**—the **fire from 1952,** the **hidden newspaper clipping,** and the worst part...

Someone else had been there.

Watching.

Another Secret Note

Just as Ariana was lost in thought, her **broom hit something solid.**

Thunk!

She frowned and bent down.

A **folded piece of paper** was wedged under the lockers near the classroom doors.

It was **yellowed with age,** barely visible against the **dusty floor.**

Ariana's **heart skipped.**

She quickly pulled it out and unfolded it.

The familiar, **old-fashioned handwriting** sent a **shiver** through her.

"R.M."

Riya Mehra.

Another clue.

Before she could read further, **Tara leaned in over her shoulder.**

"Oooh, another ancient love letter?"

Ariana rolled her eyes. **"Yeah, because someone totally hid their love letters under dusty lockers in the 1950s."**

Tara **gasped dramatically.** "Unless… it's a ghost love letter! **A tragic romance! Midnight meetings under the—"**

Ariana shoved the letter into her pocket. **"Tara, please. Focus."**

Tara sighed. **"Fine, fine. But if there's a ghost involved, I want credit."**

Ariana **stifled a laugh**, but her mind was **racing.**

Another **clue** from **Riya Mehra.**

What had she left behind this time?

She didn't have time to figure it out yet—because **Tuesday meant bath time.**

And **bath time at St. Joanna's** was a **whole different adventure.**

The Great Bathing Room Incident

If there was one thing **every girl at St. Joanna's Convent dreaded**, it was **Tuesday bath time at 5:30 PM.**

Bathing wasn't an **everyday luxury**—each girl got exactly **one day a week**, one **stall**, and **one half-bucket of hot water** fetched from the **common tap outside.**

And once inside, you had **exactly thirty minutes.**

Go past that? The **matrons would start banging on the doors** like police raiding a crime scene.

Ariana **hurried toward the bathing area**, juggling her **tin bucket of hot water** as she dodged girls rushing past her.

Tara **grinned.** "Thirty minutes of **pure relaxation.**"

Ariana snorted. **"You mean thirty minutes of extreme time management."**

She reached her **stall**, quickly **mixed the hot and cold water**, and poured the **first mug over her head.**

Finally, a **moment of peace.**

And then—

Something **moved.**

Ariana froze.

It wasn't the sound of **someone walking.**

It was **above her.**

A strange, subtle **shuffling.**

Her **stomach flipped.**

The bathing stalls had **high walls**, but the **ceilings were open**—and **someone was up there.**

Slowly, Ariana **tilted her head back.**

And that's when she saw it.

A **head.**

Peeping down at her from above.

For **one horrifying second**, she stared into a pair of **wide, guilty eyes.**

Then—

Ariana screamed.

"OI! WHAT THE—?!"

The head **vanished immediately.** A **loud thud** followed as the person scrambled to **climb down.**

Furious, Ariana **grabbed her towel**, wrapped herself up, and **stormed out of the stall**—just in time to see a **familiar figure sprinting down the hallway.**

Ariana **took off after her.**

Tara, who had just **come out of her stall** with a towel on her head, blinked. **"Why are you running? Why is she running? WHY IS EVERYONE RUNNING?!"**

Ariana caught up to the culprit near the **dormitory hallway** and **grabbed her wrist.**

"You have three seconds to explain yourself before I dunk you in the sock bucket."

The girl **turned, looking like a trapped rabbit.**

It was **Rita.**

A **junior from Class 7.**

Ariana **narrowed her eyes.** "Explain. Now."

Rita **stammered.** "I—I was looking for my soap!"

Ariana **folded her arms. "From the ceiling?"**

Rita **gulped.** "Uh… it… it fell **up** there?"

Ariana **stared at her.** "You want to try that sentence again?"

Rita's **face turned red.** "I—I was just curious! I didn't mean to—"

"Peep into my stall like a complete creep?" Ariana finished for her.

Rita **winced.** "It's just… everyone says you and Tara are always sneaking around. You're always up to something! I just… wanted to see what was so special about you."

Ariana **raised an eyebrow.** "And your best idea was to **climb the bathing stalls** and **stare at me mid-shampoo?"**

Rita **gave a nervous giggle. "When you say it like that… it sounds weird."**

"That's because it IS weird."

Tara finally **caught up,** panting. **"Did… you just… chase someone… in a towel?"**

Ariana **exhaled** and let go of Rita. **"You're lucky I don't have time to deal with you. But if you try that again—"**

"**I won't! I swear!**" Rita **held up her hands.**

Ariana sighed. **"Go. Before I change my mind."**

Rita **sprinted off.**

Tara watched her disappear, then **turned to Ariana.**

"What even was that?"

Ariana **shook her head.** "I don't know. But something tells me **she's not the only one watching us."**

Tara frowned. **"You think this was just some junior being nosy?"**

Ariana glanced at her pocket, where the **old letter from Riya Mehra** was still hidden.

"I'm not sure," she murmured. **"But I intend to find out."**

CHAPTER 12

Drying in the Sun & Secret Notes

Silence is Golden (Except When You're Starving)

Sunday afternoons at **St. Joanna's Convent** were built on **discipline.**

And **discipline meant rules.**

One of the most **sacred, unbreakable** rules?

□ NO TALKING IN THE LINE. □

It didn't matter if you were **lining up for food, chapel, or even the bathroom**—the nuns had **razor-sharp hearing** and could detect a whisper from **across the entire school.**

But here's the **real problem.**

Sunday afternoons also meant one thing—hunger.

After **morning mass, choir practice, and an entire day of being 'holy,'** the only thing anyone could think about was **lunch.**

And this particular Sunday, the food smelled **heavenly.**

Plates of **steaming rice, golden fried potatoes, dal thick with ghee**—all waiting inside the **senior refectory.**

All they had to do was **wait in silence.**

Easy, right?

Wrong.

A few juniors couldn't resist. A whisper here, a suppressed giggle there.

And then—

BOOM.

"YOU ALL DRY IN THE SUN!"

Sister Agnes's voice **thundered** across the courtyard.

A **horrified silence** fell over the entire senior school.

Ariana felt her **soul leave her body.**

Tara grabbed her arm in **mute panic.**

The **refectory doors?** **Slammed shut.** The **food?** Right there inside. But **them?** Stranded **outside.**

Under the **blazing afternoon sun.**

Hundreds of students stood frozen, **eyes darting around like panicked deer.**

One girl **clutched her stomach dramatically,** as if she could already feel **starvation setting in.**

Someone behind Ariana **muttered in despair.**

Tara turned to Ariana and **whispered through gritted teeth,** "Tell my parents I loved them."

Ariana sighed. **"Shut up, Tara."**

The Strategy of Eating in the Refectory

After what felt like an **eternity of suffering** (but was actually just **15 minutes** of sun-drying and regret), **Sister Agnes finally relented.**

The doors **swung open.**

The **entire senior school** marched in silently, heads down, **humbled by their suffering.**

Ariana sat down, mentally **thanking every saint she could name.**

Finally. Food.

But, of course, **there were more rules.**

☐ **First Bell:** You could **get up** to grab your **pickles, ghee, and anything extra.**

This was a **survival moment.**

The **brave and the fast** would get the **best pickles.** The **slow and the unfortunate** would be left with **pickle oil and sadness.**

Ariana **sprinted** to the table, **grabbing the last big chunk of mango pickle.**

A junior next to her sighed **in defeat.**

Ariana gave her a **sympathetic nod. "You have to be quicker next time, kid."**

She and Tara returned to their seats just in time for the **second bell.**

□ **Now talking was forbidden.** □ **Eating speed was encouraged.**

Tara nudged Ariana and **whispered with a grin,** "Only at St. Joanna's do we have a **bell to start eating,** a **bell to get pickles,** and a **bell to stop talking.** It's like a **well-organized food orchestra!"**

Ariana smirked. **"And the conductor is Sister Agnes."**

Tara **snorted into her dal.**

Sister Agnes **glared at them.**

Ariana quickly **picked up her spoon** and pretended to be the **most obedient student in school history.**

A Mysterious Note

Just as Ariana took her **last bite,** something **fluttered into her lap.**

A **folded piece of paper.**

Her **heart stopped.**

She **looked around.**

No one was looking at her.

Slowly, she **unfolded the note.**

The same **elegant, old-fashioned handwriting.**

"Meet me behind the chapel. Midnight."

Ariana's **pulse quickened.**

Another **clue.**

Another **secret.**

Another **late-night adventure.**

Tara, noticing her expression, **raised an eyebrow.** "What now?"

Ariana **tucked the note into her pocket** and whispered, **"Looks like we're sneaking out again."**

Tara **groaned.** "Of course we are. **Why do I even ask?"**

Ariana **smiled.**

Because this **mystery was far from over.**

CHAPTER 13

Midnight Secrets at the Chapel

A Risky Meeting

The **wind howled** through the trees as Ariana and Tara **tiptoed across the school grounds**, hearts **pounding.**

It was **midnight.**

And they were sneaking towards the **chapel.**

Just as the **mysterious note** had instructed.

"Remind me why I always let you talk me into this?" Tara muttered.

"Because you love adventure," Ariana whispered back.

"I love sleeping more," Tara grumbled.

The **chapel loomed ahead,** its **white walls glowing eerily** under the moonlight.

The school was silent—**too silent.**

Ariana clenched the **note** in her pocket.

"Meet me behind the chapel. Midnight."

Who had sent it?

Neel? A friend? **An enemy?**

They reached the **back of the chapel** and waited.

The night stretched on, filled only with the **distant chirping of crickets.**

Nothing.

Tara sighed. **"I knew this was a bad ide—"**

CRACK.

A branch **snapped.**

Ariana **spun around.**

A **shadow** moved near the trees.

"Who's there?" she whispered.

A figure **stepped forward.**

Neel.

His face was **tense**, his eyes **darting around** as if checking if they were alone.

"Ariana, you shouldn't be here," he said in a low voice.

"You sent the note?" she asked.

Neel **shook his head. "No. But I need to tell you something."**

Ariana's **stomach tightened.**

If **he hadn't sent the note**… then **who had?**

Tara grabbed her arm. **"I don't like this. We should go."**

Neel **ignored her.** He leaned in.

"It's about Riya."

Ariana **froze.**

Neel exhaled sharply. **"She found something hidden in the school. Something that someone didn't want her to find."**

Ariana's **heart pounded.**

"Then she disappeared?" she asked.

Neel nodded. **"And after that, no one ever talked about her again."**

Ariana's **stomach twisted.**

This wasn't just a mystery anymore.

Someone had **erased Riya Mehra from St. Joanna's history.**

And now—

they were watching Ariana, too.

CHAPTER 14

The Snake at the Pavilion

—•—

A Hidden Message

The **next morning**, Ariana was **still shaken** from the night before.

The **shadowy figure.**

Neel's **warning.**

The fact that **someone had erased Riya Mehra from history.**

And now, someone was **watching them.**

"Who was that mystery figure?" Tara asked, stuffing a handful of toast into her mouth at breakfast.

Ariana **poked at her food.** "I don't know. But I don't like how this is going."

Tara swallowed. "Okay, but what's the plan? We can't just… walk up to Sister Agnes and say, 'Excuse me, were you covering up a scandal in 1952?'"

Ariana smirked. "No, but I'd pay to see you try."

Tara sighed dramatically. "I hate how much you enjoy dragging me into your detective nonsense."

Ariana **pulled out Riya's last letter.**

"There is something hidden within these walls. A secret buried long before our time."

Ariana **tapped the words.** "We need to start looking in places no one else thinks about."

Tara frowned. **"Like?"**

Ariana **looked around.**

Her **eyes landed on the red-roofed pavilion**—a long **sheltered seating area** where students often **read, gossiped, or passed time.**

She squinted.

Something about it felt… **off.**

Then she noticed—one of the **wooden beams was different from the others.**

A Trap from the Past

Ariana **stood on a bench** and ran her fingers along the **beam's surface.**

Her **fingertips brushed against something rough.**

"Ariana, what are you doing?" Tara asked, watching her like she'd lost her mind.

"There's something here."

She pushed at the **loose beam.**

It creaked—then **shifted slightly.**

Ariana's **heart pounded.**

She reached up and wiggled the **wooden plank again.**

Suddenly—

Something **heavy** dropped from the roof.

Right in front of her.

A **SNAKE.**

Tara let out a **blood-curdling scream.**

Ariana **stumbled backward,** her breath **caught in her throat.**

The snake **coiled,** its scales **glistening** in the sunlight.

For a **terrifying second,** no one moved.

Then—

The snake **slithered away** into the grass.

Silence.

Ariana and Tara **looked at each other, pale.**

Tara **gasped for breath.** "I—I think I died for a second."

Ariana's **legs were still shaking.**

But she wasn't looking at the **snake anymore.**

She was looking at the **hollow space inside the loosened beam.**

A **small, rolled-up paper** was stuffed inside.

Ariana reached up and **pulled it out, hands trembling.**

Tara **stared.** "Please tell me that's not another clue. I need a moment to recover."

Ariana **unrolled the paper.**

The **handwriting was familiar.**

Riya Mehra's.

"If you're reading this, I hope you're braver than I was."

Ariana's **stomach flipped.**

Riya had **left this message hidden in the pavilion.**

But **why?**

And **what had she been so afraid of?**

Tara peeked over Ariana's shoulder. **"Ariana. I swear. If this leads to more danger, I'm quitting."**

Ariana **clenched the paper in her hands.**

They were getting **closer.**

But the **closer they got...**

The more **dangerous it became.**

CHAPTER 15

Whispers in the Dark

A Restless Night

The **pavilion incident** haunted Ariana's mind.

The **snake.**

The **hidden message.**

The way Riya's note sounded more like a **warning than a clue.**

"If you're reading this, I hope you're braver than I was."

What had **Riya** been **so afraid of?**

Ariana **lay on her dormitory bed,** staring at the ceiling.

Something felt… **off.**

Her **body ached,** her stomach **twisted in a way she couldn't explain.**

She turned **uncomfortably.**

Was it because of the **mystery?**

Or… was something else **wrong?**

She **didn't know.**

What she **did** know was that she was **thirsty.**

Ariana reached for her **empty water bottle** on the bedside table and sighed.

Of course. **No water.**

The dormitory rule was **clear—no carrying water inside because of the wooden floors.**

If she wanted **water**, she'd have to **go to the tap outside.**

Ariana glanced at Tara, who was **snoring softly.**

Carefully, she **slipped out of bed,** wrapped her **shawl around her shoulders**, and **tiptoed toward the door.**

The corridor was **silent** except for the soft **creaks of the wooden floor** beneath her feet.

She reached the **old metal tap near the dormitory entrance** and turned it on.

Water **gushed out**, cold against her hands.

She leaned forward to take a sip.

And then—

She heard it.

A whisper.

Soft. Quick. **Like someone murmuring nearby.**

Ariana **froze.**

She wasn't **alone.**

Her **breath caught** as she turned her head **slowly toward the corridor.**

A **shadow moved.**

Her **pulse skyrocketed.**

Was it a **teacher? A matron?**

Or worse…

Was it the **same person** who had been **watching her all this time?**

She stayed **completely still.**

Listening.

Nothing.

Then—

Another **whisper.**

The **hairs on her neck stood up.**

She wasn't **imagining it.**

Someone was **there.**

Ariana stepped **backward,** her heartbeat **thundering in her ears.**

And then, just as suddenly as it started—

The **whispering stopped.**

The **corridor was empty.**

Ariana let out a **shaky breath.**

She wasn't sure if she had just **escaped danger—**

Or if she had just been **warned.**

CHAPTER 16

The First Time

The next morning, Ariana still felt… strange.

She woke up **tired, sore, and uneasy.** The whispers from the previous night echoed in her head. Had she imagined them?

She was still thinking about it when she got out of bed—

And that's when she saw it.

A dark stain on her tunic.

Her stomach dropped.

Before she could even process it, a senior girl passing by paused, lowering her voice.

"Ariana," she whispered. "I think you need to change."

Heat rushed to Ariana's face. Embarrassment burned in her chest. What was happening?

Tara, noticing her expression, leaned in. **"Are you okay?"**

Ariana nodded quickly, though she felt anything but okay. Awkward and exposed, she hurried to the dormitory, confusion swirling inside her.

Sister Beatrice was by the window, mending a torn bedsheet.

Ariana hesitated. Then, gathering her courage, she whispered, **"Sister... I think something's wrong with me."**

Sister Beatrice looked up, immediately understanding.

Her face softened. **"Come, child,"** she said gently. **"You're growing up now."**

Growing up?

Ariana's throat felt dry as she listened carefully to Sister Beatrice's explanation.

"It happens to all young girls at some point," the nun reassured her.

Ariana nodded slowly, still overwhelmed.

Then—

Sister Beatrice clapped her hands together. **"Alright, girls! We need some pads for Ariana!"**

Before Ariana could react, the dormitory **burst into action.** Girls rummaged through their belongings, handing her pads one by one.

A small pile started forming in front of her.

Ariana **stared.** She hadn't expected this.

For something so **shocking and personal**, everyone treated it like just another ordinary part of life.

Tara grinned. **"Well, now you have enough pads to last a lifetime."**

Ariana **laughed,** the tension finally melting away.

She wasn't alone.

And maybe… just maybe… growing up wouldn't be so bad after all.

CHAPTER 17

The Tournament &
The Unexpected Message

The School Comes Alive

St. Joanna's Convent had seen many exciting days, but nothing compared to **the throwball tournament.**

For weeks, the school buzzed with anticipation. Teams from **Kurseong, Darjeeling, and other nearby schools** had arrived that morning, filling the air with electric energy.

Banners draped from balconies, students in neatly pressed uniforms cheered from the stands, and the thrill of competition **crackled** through the air.

Ariana stood at the scorekeeping table, grinning as she carefully wrote the latest scores in chalk.

St. Joanna's – 8 points.

Kurseong – 6 points.

Tara bounced beside her, eyes glued to the court. **"If we win this match, we're in the finals!"**

Ariana nodded. **"And if we win the finals…"**

"We get the trophy back!" Tara finished excitedly.

This wasn't just about winning. **It was about pride. About legacy. About defending their school's honor.**

The referee blew the whistle.

The match **exploded** with action—players diving, jumping, blocking. The crowd **roared** with every point.

Then—match point.

St. Joanna's captain leaped high, her hands striking the ball with perfect force.

It **slammed** into the opponent's court. **Unreachable.**

The final whistle blew.

"St. Joanna's wins!"

The stands **erupted.**

Ariana jumped up in excitement, nearly **dropping the chalk.**

Tara grabbed her arm. **"We're in the finals! WE'RE IN THE FINALS!"**

Ariana beamed. **This.** This was what it felt like to win a battle.

And they weren't done yet.

Ariana's Bell-Ringing Trick (And How It Backfires)

With **tournament fever in full swing,** the school had turned into a battlefield of competition.

Ariana, however, had **a secret weapon.**

She was in charge of **ringing the school bell.**

And sometimes, if a class was dragging on too long…

She rang it **five minutes early.**

Tara smirked. **"We're ending History class early today, aren't we?"**

Ariana grinned. **"You know me too well."**

With a quick glance around, she grabbed the rope and **pulled.**

The bell rang.

Success.

Within seconds, students **began packing up,** teachers glanced at the clocks, and classrooms emptied.

Ariana smirked, about to walk away—

Until someone cleared their throat behind her.

Her stomach **dropped.**

Slowly, she turned.

Sister Agnes stood there. **Arms crossed.**

Ariana swallowed.

Busted.

A Strange Note Appears

Later that evening, as tournament excitement still buzzed through the school, Ariana returned to the dormitory—

And **froze.**

A small, folded **paper lay on her bed.**

Her breath caught.

She looked around. No one was nearby.

Slowly, she picked it up and unfolded it.

The handwriting was old. **Familiar.**

Riya Mehra's.

"If you're still searching, meet me at the old chapel steps. Midnight."

Ariana's heartbeat **quickened.**

Another note. Another clue.

But... **how?**

Riya had disappeared **years ago.**

So how was she still leaving messages?

And more importantly...

Who else knew about them?

CHAPTER 18

A Christmas to Remember

The Christmas season at St. Joanna's was a strange mix of **final exams and holiday excitement.**

On one hand, students were **buried in books**, surviving their last papers.

On the other… Christmas fever had already begun.

Trunks lined the hallways. Carol practice filled the common rooms. And soon, **Santa Claus would arrive—on the school bus.**

Santa Claus Arrives!

Loud cheers **erupted** from the school grounds.

Ariana and Tara, who had been **pretending to study,** rushed outside.

The school bus crawled across the field.

At the front—**dressed in red, waving excitedly—was** this year's Santa.

Sweets flew into the air.

Students **screamed, chasing the bus.**

"GET THE CHOCOLATES!" Tara yelled, grabbing Ariana's wrist.

Ariana laughed, **catching toffees mid-air.**

Tara sprinted toward a lollipop near the bushes. **"I NEED TO BE FIRST!"**

Ariana shook her head. **"Slow down, Tara, this isn't the Olympics."**

Tara ignored her, **dramatically diving for the candy.**

Ariana **grinned.**

These were the moments that made **St. Joanna's home.**

CHAPTER 19

The Spirit Game

A Mischievous Idea

"Are we seriously doing this?" Tara whispered as she and Ariana **crept behind the old study hall** during their free time.

"Obviously," Ariana whispered back, **grinning.**

The plan was simple.

A few girls from their dorm had gathered **to perform a séance.**

Not a real one, of course. Just **for fun,** to create a little **drama.**

The goal?

To ask the **"spirits"** who stole someone's muffler last week.

Mira, the **most dramatic girl in their group**, sat cross-legged on the floor, carefully placing an **upturned glass** in the center of a large notebook.

The letters **A to Z** and **YES/NO** were scribbled on it.

"Alright," Mira whispered. "We call upon the spirits!"

Ariana **bit her lip to keep from laughing.**

The girls **placed their fingers lightly on the glass.**

Tara smirked. "Spirits, tell us… who stole Rupa's muffler?"

For a moment, **nothing happened.**

Then—**Mira's finger twitched**.

The glass **moved slightly.**

Ariana exchanged a **knowing glance** with Tara.

They weren't actually calling spirits. **Mira was totally pushing the glass.**

But that was the whole fun of it.

The girls **gasped dramatically.**

"It's moving!"

"OH MY GOD!"

"Spirits, give us a name!" Mira said in a deep, eerie voice.

The glass **slowly slid to a letter.**

'S'

Then 'H'

Then 'I'

"It's Shilpa!" someone screamed.

Ariana **almost laughed out loud** as Shilpa **turned red.**

"I DIDN'T STEAL ANYTHING!" she shrieked.

The girls **collapsed in laughter.**

It was **total nonsense**, but that's what made it fun.

An Unexpected Twist...

The game continued, and after **falsely accusing** a few more girls for fun, Mira leaned in.

"Let's ask the spirits something else."

Ariana raised an eyebrow. "Like what?"

Mira smirked. "Something spooky."

Tara, ever the troublemaker, grinned. "Let's ask... about Riya Mehra."

Ariana's heart **skipped a beat.**

For a moment, **no one spoke.**

Mira's grin faded slightly. "Okaaay... that's a bit creepy."

But the curiosity had **already spread** through the group.

"Let's do it," Rupa whispered.

Ariana hesitated. This had been a **harmless game** until now.

But something about **Riya's name** being spoken like this **felt strange.**

Still, she played along. "Alright, let's ask."

They placed their fingers back on the glass.

Mira cleared her throat and spoke in **an overly dramatic voice.**

"Spirits… tell us… what happened to Riya Mehra?"

Silence.

The wind **rustled through the trees.**

The girls **leaned in closer, waiting.**

The glass **moved slightly.**

Ariana's stomach **tightened.**

Was Mira moving it?

The glass slid.

First to **Y**

Then to **E**

Then to **S.**

The girls **squealed.**

"OH MY GOD!"

Tara giggled. "Wow, the spirits really want us to know!"

Mira smirked. "Okay, let's ask another question. Where is Riya Mehra now?"

Ariana rolled her eyes. **Mira was definitely moving it.**

The glass **moved again.**

First to **C.**

Then to **H.**

Then—

The glass **stopped.**

Ariana frowned. "Mira, why'd you stop?"

Mira blinked. "I didn't."

Silence.

A soft **creak** echoed through the old study hall.

Ariana **looked around.**

The glass **suddenly jerked** to the side—so fast that their fingers slipped off.

The girls **screamed.**

Ariana's breath **caught in her throat.**

Tara **jumped up.** "OKAY, NOPE. WE ARE DONE."

"WHO MOVED IT?!" Shilpa shrieked.

Mira **held up her hands.** "Not me!"

For the first time, Ariana realized—**Mira's fingers hadn't been on the glass when it moved.**

A cold shiver ran down her spine.

The girls **bolted** from the study hall, giggling and shrieking.

Only Ariana stayed behind for a second, staring at the **notebook where the game had ended.**

The letters were still there.

C. H.

What was it trying to spell?

Ariana swallowed and **closed the notebook.**

Whether it was **a game or something real...**

She didn't know anymore.

CHAPTER 20

The Secret Behind C.h.

The **study hall** was **empty now**, but Ariana could still feel the **energy from the planchette session lingering in the air.**

She stared at the notebook, her fingers tracing the two letters that had appeared before the game had **ended in chaos.**

C. H.

What did it mean?

A person's initials? A place? A warning?

Her heart was **still racing.** Maybe Mira had been faking the game—**but had she really moved the glass at the end?**

Something about this felt **too real.**

Footsteps echoed from the corridor outside.

Ariana **snapped the notebook shut** and turned.

Tara stood at the doorway, arms crossed. **"I swear, Ariana, if you're about to tell me the spirits actually spoke, I will pass out right now."**

Ariana exhaled. "No, but..."

She hesitated.

Should she tell Tara about the **letters that had appeared?**

Something inside her told her to **wait.**

Not yet.

Instead, she forced a grin. "You're right. It was probably Mira messing around."

Tara let out a dramatic sigh of relief. "Good. Because if that was real, I'd have already packed my bags and transferred schools."

Ariana **laughed,** but deep inside, she couldn't shake the feeling that the game had revealed **something important.**

Something she needed to figure out.

And fast.

THE CLUE NO ONE NOTICED

Later that night, back in the **dormitory,** Ariana lay in bed, **wide awake.**

She kept going over the past few weeks.

The **diary from Riya Mehra.**

The **mysterious notes.**

The **strange watcher** following her and Tara.

And now, the **planchette session spelling out "C. H."**

What was it leading to?

Her **eyes wandered** around the dormitory. Most of the girls were **asleep**, but some were still **whispering quietly,** too excited about the upcoming vacation to rest.

Ariana turned on her side, staring at the **dim light streaming in through the windows.**

And then—

Her eyes landed on something.

Her **trunk.**

She had been so distracted by the mystery that she hadn't even **finished packing for winter vacation.**

She sighed, sitting up and reaching for the lid.

She had barely lifted it when—

Something **caught her eye.**

On the **inside of the trunk lid, scratched faintly into the wood, were two letters.**

C. H.

Ariana **froze.**

Her breath hitched as she **traced the letters with her fingers.**

They had been there this whole time—**and she had never noticed.**

She swallowed hard.

This couldn't be a coincidence.

Someone—**maybe even Riya Mehra herself**—had scratched these letters into the trunk.

But why?

Her mind **raced.**

C. H.

Could it be a place?

Then, **it hit her.**

C. H. = Chapel Hall.

Her heart **pounded in her chest.**

The old **chapel hall**—the one near the main building that wasn't used often anymore.

It was mostly for **storage now.** But what if Riya had **hidden something there?**

Ariana's hands **shook** as she closed the trunk, her mind made up.

She was going to find out.

Tomorrow.

Before she left for vacation.

A DANGEROUS DISCOVERY

The next evening, just before **sunset,** Ariana made her way toward the **chapel hall.**

The air was crisp, the sky painted in **streaks of orange and pink.**

Most of the students were **busy with last-minute packing,** and teachers were **preparing for the final Christmas mass.**

This was her chance.

She slipped inside the **quiet, dusty hall.**

It smelled like **old books, wooden pews, and forgotten history.**

The stained-glass windows cast eerie patterns on the floor, making the space feel almost… **haunted.**

Ariana **steeled herself.**

She ran her hands along the wooden benches, checking for anything out of place.

Nothing.

Then, she moved to the **far corner,** where old trunks and furniture were stacked.

She pulled aside a heavy, dust-covered chair—

And **froze.**

Behind it, **half-hidden under a pile of discarded hymn books,** was something that didn't belong.

A small wooden box.

Ariana's **heart pounded.**

She **knelt down,** brushing away the dust, and slowly lifted the lid.

Inside, there was **a bundle of letters.**

Yellowed, fragile... **and addressed to Riya Mehra.**

Ariana's hands trembled as she picked up the top letter and unfolded it.

The ink was faded, but the words were still clear.

And as she read, her **blood ran cold.**

THE LETTER THAT CHANGED EVERYTHING

"Riya,

Stop asking questions. You don't know what you're getting yourself into.

If you don't stop, something will happen. And no one will be able to help you.

This is your last warning.

Leave it alone."

There was no signature.

No name.

Just **a warning.**

Ariana's **heart pounded in her ears.**

This letter was **proof** that Riya had been threatened.

Someone had wanted her to **stop investigating.**

And now, Ariana was **following the exact same path.**

She suddenly felt **very aware of how alone she was.**

The chapel hall was **too quiet.** The shadows seemed **too long.**

She had to get out of there.

Clutching the letters, she turned—

And **stopped cold.**

Because standing in the doorway—**watching her—was a shadowy figure.**

Ariana's breath **caught in her throat.**

The figure didn't move.

Didn't speak.

Just **stood there.**

Watching.

Ariana's grip on the letters **tightened.**

She wasn't supposed to be here.

And whoever this was—**they knew it.**

She took a slow step back.

The figure shifted.

Ariana's pulse **skyrocketed.**

Then, without thinking—**she ran.**

CHAPTER 21

The Chase in the Chapel Hall

Ariana's **heartbeat slammed in her chest.**

The **shadowy figure** stood in the doorway, blocking her exit.

The dim light from the stained-glass windows barely illuminated their face, but she could tell—**they were watching her.**

Waiting.

She clutched the **bundle of letters from Riya Mehra,** her palms sweaty.

Whoever they were, they knew she had found **something important.**

And they weren't happy about it.

Ariana's **mind raced.**

Should she scream? Should she run?

Before she could decide—**the figure took a step forward.**

Ariana **bolted.**

RACING THROUGH THE DARK

She **darted to the side**, weaving through the old wooden benches, her shoes **slapping against the dusty floor.**

Her breath came in **quick gasps** as she **clutched the letters to her chest.**

The figure **moved fast.**

Footsteps **echoed behind her** as she sprinted toward the **side exit.**

Locked.

Her stomach **lurched.**

The only way out was **past them.**

Ariana spun around, heart hammering. **They were closer now.**

She couldn't see their face. Only their **dark silhouette moving toward her.**

Think, Ariana. Think!

Her eyes darted to the side.

An **old wooden ladder** leaned against the wall near the choir balcony.

A risky escape… but her only chance.

She **ran toward it, gripping the ladder** and scrambling up as fast as she could.

Below, the figure hesitated.

Ariana reached the top, pulling herself onto the **dusty wooden platform.**

She turned back, expecting the person to **climb after her.**

But they didn't.

Instead, they just **stood there. Watching.**

Ariana's **chest heaved.**

Then, the figure **did something chilling.**

They raised a hand—

And pressed a **finger to their lips.**

Shhh.

Ariana's blood **ran cold.**

Before she could react, the figure **turned and disappeared into the shadows.**

WHAT JUST HAPPENED?

Ariana stayed **frozen on the choir balcony, gripping the letters.**

What… was that?

Not a teacher. Not a student.

Then who?

A **warning? A message? A threat?**

Her hands **shook.**

She looked down at the letters, her mind spinning.

This wasn't a joke anymore.

Someone knew she was looking for **Riya's truth.**

And they **wanted her to stop.**

But the question was—**why?**

THE SECRET HIDING PLACE

She waited a few more minutes, making sure the person was **gone**, before climbing down carefully.

Her legs were **wobbly,** but she forced herself to move.

She had to **hide these letters** before she returned to the dormitory.

Somewhere **safe.**

She spotted an **old confession booth** near the back of the chapel.

Perfect.

Ariana **rushed toward it,** pulled open the wooden panel inside, and **tucked the letters into a hidden gap.**

For now, they would **stay there.**

No one would find them.

Not until she figured out **who she could trust.**

BACK IN THE DORMITORY

By the time she returned to her dorm, the **usual chatter and laughter had died down.**

Most girls were already **in bed**, whispering about **Christmas break.**

Ariana felt **disconnected from it all.**

She **crawled into her bed**, staring at the ceiling.

Tara, who had been **reading under her blanket**, peeked at her.

"You okay?" she whispered.

Ariana hesitated.

Should she tell Tara about what had just happened?

The **letters, the shadowy figure, the chase in the chapel?**

Her heart said yes.

But her gut said no.

For now, she forced a **small smile.** "Yeah. Just tired."

Tara studied her for a second before **nodding.** "You're acting weird, but okay."

Ariana sighed, turning away.

She was acting weird.

Because something **wasn't right.**

And she wasn't sure who to trust anymore.

A FINAL WARNING

Just as she was about to drift off to sleep, a cold **gust of wind** made her shiver.

She turned toward the **dormitory window.**

It was slightly **open.**

Frowning, she slid out of bed and walked over.

Maybe someone had forgotten to close it?

She reached for the window—

And **stopped.**

A small, folded **piece of paper** had been **tucked into the window latch.**

Her pulse **spiked.**

She carefully **pulled it out,** unfolded it, and read the **single line written inside.**

"Stop looking, Ariana. Before it's too late."

Ariana's **breath caught in her throat.**

Someone had **been here.**

Watching.

Waiting.

And now, they had left a **warning.**

Ariana clenched the note in her fist.

She had **two choices.**

Listen to the warning and stop.

Or keep going.

And find out the truth.

Her jaw tightened.

She already knew her answer.

She wasn't going to stop.

No matter what.

CHAPTER 22

The Warning & The Raffle

Ariana's fingers trembled as she unfolded the small slip of paper.

"Stop looking, Ariana. Before it's too late."

Her stomach lurched, and her heart skipped a beat. Someone had left this in her dorm window. Someone had been watching her.

She clenched the note so tightly her fingers turned white. If they thought a warning would make her stop, they clearly didn't know her at all.

THE LAST SCHOOL DAY BEFORE BREAK – THE RAFFLE

The next morning, the halls buzzed with excitement. Winter vacation was finally within reach, but Ariana hardly noticed. Her mind was still spinning, trapped in the words of the note.

"Before it's too late." The phrase echoed in her mind like a warning bell.

"Earth to Ariana!" Tara's voice cut through her thoughts. She waved her hand in front of Ariana's face, but Ariana barely registered it.

"Huh?" Ariana blinked, shaking her head.

Tara raised an eyebrow, clearly amused. "You've been in another world today. You forget what day it is?"

Ariana frowned, still disoriented. "Uh… Friday?"

Tara groaned and smirked. "No, dumbo. Raffle Day!"

Ariana blinked again, finally breaking free from the heavy fog of her thoughts. The school lobby came into view, and the sight of a crowd gathered around a long table snapped her back to reality. Sheets of raffle tickets were being handed out in stacks.

Every year, students were given tickets to sell over the break. It was more than just a fundraiser—it was an unspoken contest. The one who sold the most tickets was crowned "star student" for the term, basking in the glory until the next break.

Tara grinned, already grabbing four sheets. "This year's my year. I'm beating my record."

Ariana chuckled weakly, taking three tickets. "I'll try. Last year, I barely sold half of them."

Tara elbowed her. "Remember last year? The girl who sold the most tickets was basically treated like a celebrity."

Ariana smiled faintly. "Almost like the birthday girls."

Tara's eyes widened. "Oh my God, yes! The birthday girl life was next-level fame."

Ariana couldn't help but laugh, remembering how everyone would swarm around the birthday girl—not just for her company, but because she had sweets to hand out. It was the one day students could ditch their dull uniforms and wear their brightest dresses.

But as the laughter faded, a memory hit her, sharp and sudden.

Riya Mehra.

Her last birthday. Riya had worn a beautiful blue dress. She'd smiled, but it was a forced smile. Her eyes... they had been distant, distracted, like there was something more troubling her than her special day.

Ariana's pulse quickened.

What if Riya's birthday had been the day she found out something dangerous?

The thought hit her like a punch to the gut.

She had to check the school records.

But first—she had to return to Chapel Hall.

CHAPTER 23

The Vanishing Letters

The evening was quiet—too quiet. Ariana slipped out of the dormitory, her steps light, her heart heavy. The campus was swallowed by a creeping twilight, shadows stretching long across the grounds. Most of the students were already holed up in their rooms, eagerly waiting for vacation to start.

It was the perfect time.

She made her way toward Chapel Hall, each step driven by a mix of urgency and dread. The wind rustled the trees above, the only sound that accompanied her as she entered the chapel. The air inside was thick with the scent of aged wood and candle wax, and the faint hum of the stained-glass windows cast eerie, colorful shadows across the stone floors.

Ariana's breath came in shallow bursts. She had to hurry.

She approached the confession booth, her fingers brushing the wood. The letters—the ones she had hidden from prying eyes—were safe there last time. She slid open the panel.

Nothing.

Her breath hitched.

The letters were gone.

A chill ran down her spine. They were missing—taken.

Someone had found them.

Panic surged in her chest, and her pulse thundered in her ears. Her mind raced. Who could've—?

Footsteps.

A soft creak from behind her.

Ariana whipped around, her heart leaping in her throat. A figure stood near the entrance, dark and unmoving in the shadows.

It was Mira.

For a moment, Ariana couldn't breathe.

Mira's eyes glinted with a mix of curiosity and something darker.

"You didn't really think you could keep secrets here, did you?" Mira's voice was almost a whisper, but it carried a weight, a warning.

Ariana's hand clenched into a fist. "What did you do?"

Mira stepped forward, her expression unreadable, her voice a taunting whisper. "Sometimes, the truth is better left hidden, don't you think?"

Ariana's throat tightened. "Where are the letters, Mira?"

Mira's lips curled into a sly smile. "They're gone, Ari. And so is the mystery."

Ariana's eyes burned with frustration and fear. The truth—Riya's story—was slipping through her fingers, and Mira was the last person she wanted standing between her and the answers.

Before Ariana could react, Mira took a step back, melting into the darkness, leaving only her words hanging in the air like a challenge.

Ariana's heart hammered as the silence of the chapel closed in around her. She had to find the letters—no matter the cost.

And she was running out of time.

CHAPTER 24

Mira's Secret &
The Holi Memory

Ariana's breath caught in her throat. "Mira? What are you doing here?"

Mira stepped out from the shadows, arms crossed, her eyes cool. "I could ask you the same thing."

Ariana's heart raced. "You've been following me."

Mira didn't flinch. "Yes, but not for the reasons you think."

Ariana narrowed her eyes, trying to read her. "Start talking."

Mira hesitated, glancing at the door to the chapel as if expecting someone to come in. She leaned closer and whispered, "I think Miss Eleanor took the letters."

Ariana's stomach dropped, her mind spinning. Miss Eleanor? The strict history teacher with a reputation for never bending the rules?

"I saw her coming out of Chapel Hall this morning," Mira continued, voice low and urgent. "She was acting... strange. Like she was hiding something."

Ariana clenched her fists. That cold, calculating teacher? She'd always felt something off about her. But now—now there was proof.

"We need to check her office," Ariana said, voice steady despite the adrenaline pumping through her.

Mira nodded. "Agreed. But first... let's get out of here before someone sees us."

As they moved through the dark, empty corridors, their footsteps echoing like a countdown, Mira's voice broke the silence. "Remember Holi?"

Ariana blinked, caught off guard by the question. "What? Holi? Why would I—"

Mira smirked. "The year they wouldn't let us play with colors, so we snuck baby powder into toilet paper and had our own little fight in the courtyard."

Ariana stifled a laugh, the memory hitting her like a punch to the gut. "Oh my God. That was our version of Holi."

For a brief second, the weight of their mission lifted. The shared memory felt like a breath of fresh air. But then, reality crashed back in, cold and unyielding.

Ariana exhaled sharply. "Tomorrow night. Miss Eleanor's office. We can't wait any longer."

Mira nodded, her face hardening with resolve. "No turning back now."

CHAPTER 25

Breaking Into Miss Eleanor's Office

The next evening, the air was thick with anticipation as Ariana and Mira crept through the school's silent hallways. The sound of their footsteps barely reached their ears—most students were long asleep, unaware of the danger that loomed just around the corner.

When they reached Miss Eleanor's office, Mira was already at work, a hairpin in her hand. Ariana raised an eyebrow. "Seriously?"

Mira flashed a grin, unbothered by the suspicion in Ariana's voice. "What? You think I'd let a little thing like a locked door stop me?"

Ariana sighed, half-exasperated, half-amused. "I don't want to know."

A few moments later, the door clicked open.

The office was suffocatingly neat—every book perfectly aligned, every file in its place. No sign of anything out of the ordinary, which only made Ariana more suspicious. She opened a drawer, rifling through pens, notebooks, and the occasional stapler. Nothing.

Then, at the bottom of the last drawer, she found it.

A file. Labeled **Riya Mehra**.

Her pulse quickened as she pulled it out, her fingers trembling. She flipped it open, heart hammering in her chest.

The first page was a suspension notice.

"Riya Mehra was suspended for trespassing into restricted areas and refusing to obey instructions regarding confidential school matters."

Ariana's stomach twisted. No mention of why Riya had gone there or what she'd discovered, but it was clear now—Riya had known something, something dangerous enough to get her silenced.

Mira leaned in, her voice barely a whisper. "She found something."

Ariana nodded grimly. "And someone made sure she stayed quiet."

The weight of the words hung in the air, the truth slowly sinking in. They weren't just uncovering a mystery—they were discovering a conspiracy.

Then, suddenly—footsteps.

Ariana froze, her breath caught in her throat. Mira's eyes widened, and they both turned toward the door, panic flashing across their faces.

The footsteps were growing closer.

If they were caught—

Ariana's heart pounded in her ears. She grabbed Mira's arm, her voice barely audible, "We need to leave. Now."

But it was already too late.

CHAPTER 26

Caught in the Dark

—·•·—

Ariana and Mira barely had a second to react.

The footsteps outside the office door grew louder. Slow. Measured. Dangerous.

Ariana's pulse thundered in her ears. Whoever it was, they knew someone was inside.

Mira grabbed Ariana's wrist, her voice a low, urgent whisper. "We have to hide."

There was no time to think. Ariana's eyes raced around the dimly lit office.

Then—her gaze landed on it. A tall, wooden cupboard at the back of the room.

Without a word, they slipped inside, pulling the door shut just as the office door swung open.

Ariana held her breath.

Through the narrow gap in the cupboard door, she saw a figure step into the room.

Miss Eleanor.

Her sharp heels clicked against the floor, the sound piercing the thick silence. She froze, eyes sweeping the room, scanning every corner as though she could sense something was off.

Ariana's muscles tensed. Her body went rigid, every fiber of her being screaming to stay still.

Miss Eleanor moved toward her desk, her footsteps slow and deliberate.

Ariana's heart hammered in her chest, louder with each passing second.

The teacher opened the bottom drawer of her desk.

Ariana's blood ran cold.

She's checking the file. She knows.

Miss Eleanor let out a slow, controlled breath. Her lips barely moved as she whispered, "I warned you."

A chill raced down Ariana's spine. She wasn't speaking to anyone in the room.

She was speaking to the file.

Riya Mehra's file.

Ariana's eyes met Mira's. Their hearts pounded in their chests. They exchanged a horrified glance, each of them silently asking the same question.

What does this mean?

Miss Eleanor slowly closed the drawer. Her fingers lingered on it for a moment, her gaze distant and unreadable. Then, without a word, she turned and walked out of the office, locking the door behind her.

The silence that followed felt like an eternity.

For three full seconds, neither of them moved.

Then, Mira exhaled sharply, her voice shaky. "Okay. That was terrifying."

Ariana swallowed hard. "She knows, Mira. She knows someone is onto her."

Mira nodded, her face hardening with determination. "Then we better figure this out before she figures us out."

Ariana's hands clenched into fists. Riya Mehra hadn't just disappeared.

She'd been silenced.

And now, they might be next.

CHAPTER 27

The Secret Room

———— •◦• ————

Back in their dormitory, Ariana and Mira sat cross-legged on the floor, the stolen suspension file spread between them.

Mira's finger traced over a faded note scrawled at the bottom of the page. "Look at this," she whispered.

Ariana leaned in, her breath catching.

There, barely visible, was a cryptic location:

C.H. - Below the Stairs.

Ariana's heart skipped a beat.

Chapel Hall.

Miss Eleanor had warned Riya to stay away from "restricted areas" before she disappeared.

And now, Ariana and Mira knew exactly where Riya had been sneaking.

Ariana's voice was barely a whisper. "We have to go back."

Mira hesitated, her gaze flickering to the window. "Ariana… what if Miss Eleanor is watching? What if—"

Ariana cut her off, her tone firm. "Then that means we're getting close."

Mira clenched her jaw, her eyes narrowing with resolve. "Okay. But this time, we go prepared."

Ariana nodded, a cold determination settling in her chest.

Tomorrow night, they were going back to Chapel Hall.

And this time, they were finding the truth. No more secrets.

CHAPTER 28

Trapped Below the School

—•—

The school was quiet, the halls bathed in darkness.

Ariana and Mira moved like shadows, their footsteps barely audible as they navigated the silent corridors. Their hearts raced, each step taking them closer to whatever lay beneath Chapel Hall.

They reached the hall, the stained-glass windows casting long, eerie shadows across the floor. Ariana's pulse quickened as she counted the steps from the entrance, each one bringing them closer to the hidden door.

And then—there it was.

A small, nearly invisible door, tucked beneath the staircase.

"This is it," Ariana whispered, her voice tight with anticipation.

Mira exhaled, tension in her shoulders. "Let's go."

Ariana pushed open the door, the hinges creaking with a sound that felt deafening in the silence. A dark, narrow passage stretched before them, the air thick and musty.

They stepped inside, the door slamming shut behind them with an ominous thud.

And then—

The floor vanished beneath their feet.

Ariana's stomach dropped as she and Mira plunged into total darkness.

CHAPTER 29

Riddles in the Dark

Ariana hit the ground with a bone-jarring thud. Pain exploded in her side, but she forced herself to her feet, coughing against the dust that filled the air.

Mira groaned beside her. "Ow. That was NOT fun."

Ariana's pulse thundered in her ears as she scrambled to her feet. "Where are we?"

Her hand fumbled for her phone, the flashlight's weak beam cutting through the thick darkness. It illuminated a massive underground room, its vastness stretching beyond what the light could reach.

Ariana's breath hitched as her eyes swept over the room—books, papers, old maps, all piled high and untouched. And then—

Her heart froze.

A wall covered in newspaper clippings.

Missing Student: Riya Mehra.

Secrets Buried Under St. Mary's School.

Mira sucked in a breath beside her. "Oh my God… this is—"

Ariana stepped forward, her eyes scanning the headlines, heart pounding as she processed the familiar names and places. But then—she stopped.

A crumpled letter was pinned to the wall, hanging precariously as if it held the answers they needed.

With trembling hands, Ariana reached for it, her fingers brushing the brittle paper. She opened it carefully, and when she read the first few lines, her blood ran cold.

It was a confession.

From Miss Eleanor.

"Riya, I should have warned you earlier. This school has secrets—secrets that go beyond me. You're not safe. I tried to protect you, but I was too late. If you find this… run."

Ariana's breath came fast, the words sinking into her chest like a weight she couldn't lift.

"She—she wasn't trying to hide something," Ariana whispered, her voice shaking. "She was trying to help Riya."

Mira's eyes widened. "Then who—"

A door slammed shut.

Ariana whipped around.

And standing at the entrance of the underground room—was someone they never expected.

CHAPTER 30

The Final Reveal

Ariana's heart nearly stopped.

The figure stepped forward, their face slowly illuminated by the faint glow of the flashlight.

It was the principal.

The one person they thought was safe from suspicion.

Mira gasped, her voice trembling. "You—"

The principal smiled, a cold, calculating expression that sent a shiver down Ariana's spine.

"You girls really should have stopped when I warned you."

Ariana's stomach twisted. This was the one person who had access to every student, every file, every secret in the school. The one person who controlled it all.

And now… they knew too much.

The principal's voice was calm, almost pitying. "It was never about Miss Eleanor, was it? She was just a pawn, like all of you."

Ariana's mind reeled. "You—"

She didn't get to finish the sentence.

Suddenly, Ariana grabbed Mira's hand, the urgency in her movements making everything else fade. "RUN!"

They bolted toward the exit, but the principal's voice echoed in the stillness, a cruel whisper that sliced through the night.

"You can't run from the truth, girls."

Ariana's lungs burned as they sprinted through the darkness, the weight of what they had uncovered pressing down on her chest. She didn't care.

They had the truth now.

And she wasn't going to let them bury it again.

CHAPTER 31

The Final Piece

The wind whispered through the tall trees of the school grounds, the last traces of daylight fading as Ariana and Mira stood in the shadow of the chapel, their breaths quick and shallow. The once-familiar smell of damp stone and fresh earth filled the air—this was their school, the place that held their memories. But now, it felt different. This was no longer a sanctuary; it was a place riddled with secrets.

"We're almost there," Ariana whispered, her voice trembling, not just from the cold but from the weight of the truth that loomed closer.

Mira nodded, her eyes scanning the surroundings—the old brick buildings, the green field where they once ran freely, the spot by the refectory where they'd laughed during lunch breaks. Everything seemed so innocent, so pure. But somewhere beneath it all, something dark had been hidden.

Ariana could still hear the laughter from the playground, the echoes of carefree days spent with friends, the sounds of the throwball court where they'd huddled in teams. The library, just below the senior class building, had once been a place of quiet refuge. But now, as they moved toward their final destination, those memories felt distant, as though they belonged to another life.

"This is where it all started," Ariana said, her voice barely above a whisper.

Mira's expression softened, a mix of nostalgia and determination. "Let's finish this. For Riya."

They moved swiftly toward the hidden passageway beneath the old stone bench in the pavilion, a spot that had always seemed too quiet, too secluded for the carefree students they once were. Tonight, it held the answers.

CHAPTER 32

The Secret Underground

The air was thick with tension as Ariana and Mira entered the narrow, dimly lit passage under the school grounds. The bricks beneath their feet, worn and cold, seemed to echo their every step. The path was tight and winding, like the halls of their school that they'd once explored as children, not knowing the secrets they would one day uncover.

Ariana's hand brushed the damp stone walls as they crept forward. The small stone steps led them deeper into the earth, into the very heart of St. Joanna's—a place where memories had been buried, both literal and metaphorical.

"Do you remember the old cubicles above the primary classes?" Ariana asked suddenly, the question tumbling from her lips before she could stop it.

Mira looked at her, her expression distant for a moment. "Of course. I always thought those rooms were magical. They were always so quiet, tucked away from the chaos of the playground below."

Ariana smiled, though her heart was heavy. "It feels like a lifetime ago. Now, all I can think about is what we're about to find down here."

As they reached the bottom of the stairs, a massive underground chamber spread out before them. It was colder here, the air stale with age, and the walls were lined with forgotten remnants—papers, old books, and strange markings that seemed to whisper of things long buried.

In the center of the room, a wall covered in yellowing newspaper clippings caught their attention.

"Riya Mehra," Mira breathed, stepping forward. Her voice wavered with disbelief. "It's all here."

Ariana's heart pounded as she scanned the headlines, her eyes stopping on one that made her blood run cold: *Missing Student: Riya Mehra.* Beneath it, a picture of Riya, smiling, her eyes sparkling with life.

Ariana's fingers trembled as she reached for a crumpled letter pinned to the wall. Unfolding it, her breath caught in her throat as she read:

"Riya, I should have warned you earlier. This school has secrets—secrets that go beyond me. You're not safe. I tried to protect you, but I was too late. If you find this… run."

The weight of the truth hit Ariana like a ton of bricks.

"She wasn't trying to hide it," she whispered. "She was trying to protect Riya."

CHAPTER 33

The Shocking Reveal

Suddenly, the distant sound of footsteps reached their ears—slow and deliberate. They froze, hearts racing in their chests.

Before they could react, the door to the underground chamber slammed open. And there, standing in the entrance, was a figure they never expected to see.

The principal.

Ariana's breath caught in her throat. "No," she whispered in disbelief. "It can't be…"

The principal's lips curved into a cold smile, one that didn't reach his eyes. "You girls really should have stopped when I warned you," he said, his voice echoing in the vast, cold room.

Mira's eyes widened, the realization dawning on her like a dark cloud. "You… You were behind this the whole time?"

Ariana's mind raced, her heart pounding in her chest. All this time, they had suspected the wrong person. It wasn't Miss Eleanor who had been hiding the truth—it was the principal. The one who had the power to control everything, who had access to every file, every student's life.

He had the power to make Riya Mehra disappear.

And now, Ariana and Mira knew too much.

CHAPTER 34

The Final Escape

—•—

"RUN!" Ariana shouted, grabbing Mira's hand. They turned and bolted down the narrow corridor, their footsteps echoing in the silent darkness.

Behind them, the principal's voice rang out, but they didn't look back. They couldn't.

As they ran through the passageway, the memories of their school days flooded their minds—the green field where they'd played, the old stone bench where they'd sat and talked for hours, the library where they'd studied. St. Joanna's was more than just a school—it was a part of them. A part of their childhood. And they were determined not to let it be tarnished by the secrets buried beneath its surface.

Ariana's lungs burned as they reached the exit, the faint light of the moon casting long shadows on the cold brick walls. The school grounds stretched out before them, familiar and comforting, even in the dead of night.

As they stumbled into the open, breathless but alive, Ariana knew one thing for certain: the truth would never be buried again. She had everything she needed—everything they needed—to bring the real story to light. And this time, no one could silence them.

The stories of St. Joanna's would live on, untold for too long, but finally set free.

Epilogue

The walls of St. Joanna's stood silent under the weight of time—silent, but not forgotten. Ariana stood at the edge of the field where they had once played, her fingers brushing the worn wood of the old bench. The moonlight bathed the school grounds in an ethereal glow, but this time, it wasn't just the silence of memories that filled the air. It was the weight of truth.

Years had passed since the letters were uncovered, since the whispers of the past had been forced into the light. The girls who had once been bound by secrets were now free. Free, yes—but forever changed.

Some stories, once told, can never be untold.

Ariana's heart no longer carried the heavy weight of unanswered questions. The truth had been uncovered, and with it, the past had found its voice—its own voice. It had demanded to be heard, and it had left its mark on every corner of St. Joanna's.

The truth wasn't just something to be written in books or passed down through whispered conversations. It was now a part of the air they breathed, the ground beneath their feet.

But the most unexpected part of it all?

Ariana had finally understood.

The lies weren't just buried in the halls of St. Joanna's.

They lived in the spaces we don't want to look.

In the silences we refuse to hear.

As she turned to leave, the sound of laughter echoed in the distance—girls, young and old, reclaiming their voices.

And in the cool breeze that swept through the hills, there was one final whisper. A promise.

The stories of the past were not over. They had only just begun.

Take a Pause.
One Last Thing.

I want to take a moment to thank you, from the bottom of my heart, for letting this story into your life. Every reader's journey with my book is precious to me, and if it resonated with you, I'd be truly grateful if you could share your thoughts with others. A kind review on Amazon can make a world of difference and help others discover this story.

If you'd like to stay connected, I'd love to hear from you on Instagram-just find me at @sonam_gadia_author. Your feedback, your thoughts, and your support inspire me every single day.

Thank you for being part of this journey.

With all my gratitude,

— Sonam Gadia

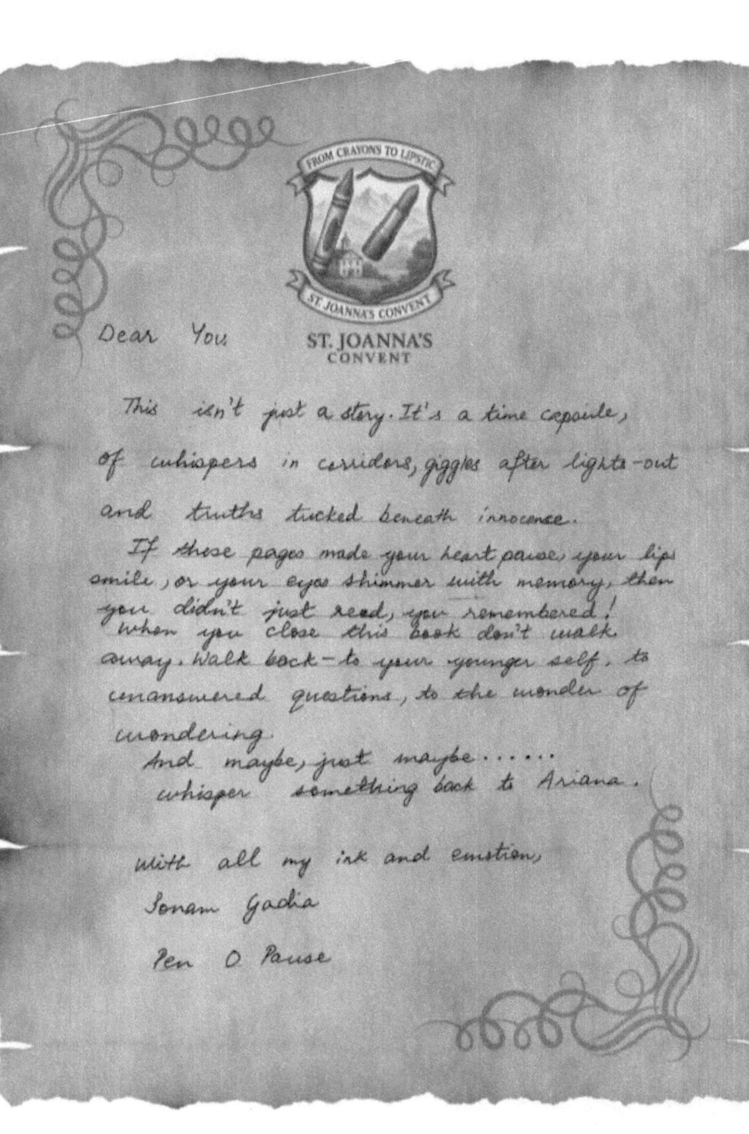

Dear You

This isn't just a story. It's a time capsule,
of whispers in corridors, giggles after lights-out
and truths tucked beneath innocence.
   If these pages made your heart pause, your lips
smile, or your eyes shimmer with memory, then
you didn't just read, you remembered!
   When you close this book don't walk
away. Walk back — to your younger self, to
unanswered questions, to the wonder of
wondering.
   And maybe, just maybe......
   whisper something back to Ariana.

With all my ink and emotion,
Sonam Gadia

Pen O Pause